Dear Parent:

Congratulations! Your child is taking the first steps on an exciting journey. The destination? Independent reading!

STEP INTO READING® will help your child get there. The program offers five steps to reading success. Each step includes fun stories and colorful art. There are also Step into Reading Sticker Books, Step into Reading Math Readers, Step into Reading Phonics Readers, Step into Reading Write-In Readers, and Step into Reading Phonics Boxed Sets—a complete literacy program with something to interest every child.

Learning to Read, Step by Step!

Ready to Read Preschool–Kindergarten
• big type and easy words • rhyme and rhythm • picture clues
For children who know the alphabet and are eager to begin reading.

Reading with Help Preschool–Grade 1
• basic vocabulary • short sentences • simple stories
For children who recognize familiar words and sound out new words with help.

Reading on Your Own Grades 1–3
• engaging characters • easy-to-follow plots • popular topics
For children who are ready to read on their own.

Reading Paragraphs Grades 2–3
• challenging vocabulary • short paragraphs • exciting stories
For newly independent readers who read simple sentences with confidence.

Ready for Chapters Grades 2–4
• chapters • longer paragraphs • full-color art
For children who want to take the plunge into chapter books but still like colorful pictures.

STEP INTO READING® is designed to give every child a successful reading experience. The grade levels are only guides. Children can progress through the steps at their own speed, developing confidence in their reading, no matter what their grade.

Remember, a lifetime love of reading starts with a single step!

Visit us on the Web!
StepIntoReading.com
www.randomhouse.com/kids

Educators and librarians, for a variety of teaching tools, visit us at www.randomhouse.com/teachers

ISBN: 978-0-7364-2813-2
Printed in the United States of America   20 19 18 17 16 15 14 13 12

STEP INTO READING®

DISNEY · PIXAR

Cars

Five Fast Tales

Step 1 and 2 Books

A Collection of Five Early Readers

Random House 🏠 New York

Contents

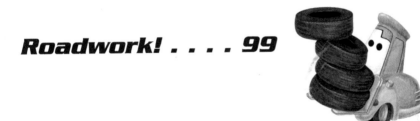

STEP INTO READING®

STEP 1

Disney · PIXAR

Cars

OLD, NEW, RED, BLUE!

By Melissa Lagonegro

Random House New York

Old truck.

New car.

Red truck.

Blue car.

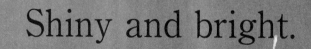

Shiny and bright.

Dull and brown.

Day on the highway.

Night in the town.

Dirty car.

Clean car.

Nice car.

Mean car.

Drive fast, fast, fast.

Drive nice and slow.

Cars ride high.

Cars ride low.

Tires are big.

Tires are small.

Piles of tires,
short and tall.

Wheels rolling
on the ground.

Cars and trucks
drive all around.

Beep, beep!

STEP INTO READING®

STEP 1

DISNEY · PIXAR
THE WORLD OF
Cars

Race Team

By Dennis R. Shealy

Illustrated by the Disney Storybook Artists

Random House ⌂ New York

Lightning McQueen
is going to a race.

Mack will take him.

All the cars get ready.

Sarge and Flo bring

cans of gas and oil.

Guido loads Fillmore
with water for Lightning.

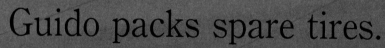

Guido packs spare tires.

Mater drives in circles.

He is excited!

The cars drive
to the race.
It is far.

Poor Guido gets tired.

Mater gives him a tow.

Big trucks rest
at the truck stop.
The cars keep going.

Mater sees
Lightning and Mack.
There are cars
all around them.

Reporters ask Lightning
about the race.
They take many pictures.

The racetrack is a
busy place!
Mack parks in the pit.

He watches Lightning

practice.

Doc puts on his headset.

It is time for the race.

Mater cheers.

He wants Lightning

to win!

The pit crew is ready.

Lightning drives
to the starting line.
His pit crew yells,
"Go, Lightning, go!"

The race starts. <u>Vroom!</u>

Lightning is in front!

He drives the fastest.

Lightning gets tired.

But he keeps going.

Lightning McQueen
wins the race!
<u>Ka-chow!</u>

The race is over.
Lightning and Mack
head home!

STEP INTO READING®

STEP 2

Disney · PIXAR

Cars

Driving Buddies

Adapted by Apple Jordan

Illustrated by the Disney Storybook Artists

Inspired by the art and character designs created by Pixar Animation Studios

Random House 🏠 New York

Lightning was

a race car.

He was shiny and fast.

He wanted one thing—
to win the big race!

Mater was a tow truck.

He was old and rusty.

He wanted one thing—
a best friend.

Mater lived
in a little town.
The streets were quiet.
All was calm.

One night,
Lightning got lost
on his way
to the big race.

He sped into
the little town.
Sheriff chased him.
Lightning got scared!

He flew into fences!

He crashed into cones!

He ripped up the road!

He made a big mess.

Lightning was
sent to jail.
He met Mater there.
Mater liked
Lightning right away.

Sally, the town lawyer,
and the other cars
wanted Lightning
to fix the road.

Lightning could not
leave town until
the job was done.

Lightning got to work.

He was unhappy.

Mater wanted
to show him some fun.

He took Lightning

tractor tipping.

It *was* fun.

Lightning told Mater
why he wanted
to win the big race.

He would have fame
and a new look.
He would be a winner!

Mater was happy.

He had

a new best friend.

Lightning fixed
the road at last!
The news reporters
found Lightning!

Mack the truck
was glad to see him!
It was time to go
to the big race.

Mater was sad
to see his buddy leave.
The other cars
were sad, too.

So Mater and his friends
went to the racetrack.
They helped Lightning.

But Lightning still
did not win.
He helped an old friend
finish the race instead.

Now he knew
that winning was not
what he wanted most.

What he wanted most
were friends.

STEP INTO READING® STEP 2

Disney · PIXAR
Cars

ROADWORK!

By Melissa Lagonegro
Illustrated by Art Mawhinney

Random House 🏠 New York

New cars are coming
to Radiator Springs.
They want to see
Lightning McQueen!

The town is
getting ready.
They have work to do!

Lightning paves the road.
It will be smooth
for his fans.

Ramone gives himself
a fresh coat of paint.

He is ready to paint
all the new cars
that come to town.

Sarge leads
his own boot camp.

He will get
all the 4x4s that visit
into good shape.

Fillmore makes
his own fuel.
He hopes
Lightning's fans
are thirsty.

At Casa Della Tires,
Luigi has
new tires to sell.
Lightning tries them on.

Guido helps, too.
He is a busy forklift.

Flo runs the diner.
Cars visit and sip oil
with friends.

Soon it will be packed
with racing fans.

Red waters the flowers.
He wants the town
to look its best!

Sally fixes up her motel.
It is the perfect place
for guests to rest.

Frank cuts
and harvests grain.
Mater gets Frank to
work extra hard.

Sheriff puts up
new road signs.

He does not want

anyone to speed.

After a long drive,
the cars need a tune-up.
Doc is ready to take
good care of them.

Lizzie gets
new bumper stickers.
She will sell them
in her shop.

Kori reports
the latest news.

Al Oft,

the Lightyear blimp,

flies overhead.

He lets everyone
in town know
when visitors are
on their way.

The town is ready
and the work is done!
The cars go out
and have some fun!

Welcome to
Radiator Springs!

DISNEP · PIXAR

Cars

The Spooky Sound

By Melissa Lagonegro

Illustrated by Ron Cohee

Random House 🏠 New York

Lightning McQueen
and Mater like to tell
spooky stories.

Their friends are scared!
But Mater and Lightning
are not.

Lightning and Mater
drive home.
Ahhhoo!
They hear
a spooky sound.

They want
to find out
what it is.

Lightning and
Mater drive by
Ramone's paint shop.
Ahhhoo!

Mater sees
a scary shape.
Is it a monster?

Lightning goes
into the shop.
He finds paint cans!
He tells Mater
there is no monster.

They drive
by Doc's shop.
It is open late.
<u>Ahhhoo!</u>

The sound is louder.
They see
sparks and flames.
Is it a fire monster?

Mater is scared.

But there is

no fire monster.

Doc is fixing Sarge.

The cars drive
to Casa Della Tires.
Ahhhoo!
The sound is closer.
Mater sees
a creepy shape.

Is it a monster
with two heads?

143

Lightning finds
tall piles of tires.
Luigi and Guido
are having a sale.

Mater and Lightning
drive into the desert.
<u>Ahhhoo!</u>

Mater sees a light
in the sky.
Is it a monster
that glows?

Lightning spots
Al Oft.
He is taking
a night flight.

Lightning and Mater
keep driving.
Ahhhoo!
The sound is right
behind them!

Mater is really scared!

Lightning wants
to find the sound.
He turns around
very slowly.

The spooky sound
is not a monster!
It does not have fire.
It does not have
two heads.

It does not glow.

It is Sheriff!

He is driving

in his sleep!

Lightning and Mater
laugh and laugh.
They are
not afraid!

But then they see

two glowing eyes!

Oh, no!

What is it?

They do not want
to find out!